Bingo and the Burblies

By Steve Howson
Illustrated by Gisela Bohorquez

Chapter 1

Bingo lived in a village in the rainforest. Her family had lived there for hundreds of years.

Bingo loved to explore. Every day she discovered something new. Like a shiny beetle with great black horns. Or a blue frog living under a leaf. Or a bright red bird with a curly tail. When she told her grandfather, he knew the names for all of them.

Bingo and the Burblies

'Bingo and the Burblies'

An original concept by Steve Howson

Illustrated by Gisela Bohorquez

Published by MAVERICK ARTS PUBLISHING LTD

Studio 3A, City Business Centre, 6 Brighton Road,

Horsham, West Sussex, RH13 5BB

+44 (0)1403 256941

A CIP catalogue record for this book is available at the British Library.

ISBN 978-1-84886-396-5

Maverick publishing

www.maverickbooks.co.uk

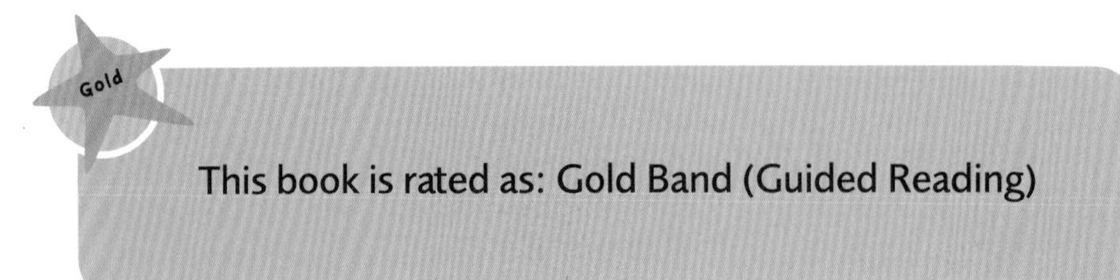

This book is rated as: Gold Band (Guided Reading)

One day Bingo wandered further than usual. She found noisy diggers working among the trees. Bingo crept past them. She followed a mighty river through the forest until it dropped over a ledge and became a huge waterfall.

Bingo climbed over the ledge and down the slippery rocks. She noticed a deep cave behind the waterfall. She couldn't resist going inside. It was gloomy and wet. The roar of falling water filled the air.

Then Bingo noticed another sound. A sort of gurgling, burbling noise. It was coming from above her head. Bingo peered into the darkness and gasped.

Four small creatures were staring back at her. They had brown furry bodies, bright orange eyes and long pink noses shaped like trumpets. Strangest of all, they had bare pink hands and feet that were covered in sticky pads.

There were two larger animals and two smaller ones.

They held each other tight and burbled at Bingo.

“I think I’m going to call you ‘burblies’,” said Bingo. “Please don’t be scared.”

She took a berry from her bag and held it out. The burblies looked at it for long time. Then the biggest burbly shot out a long pink tongue and gobbled it up. Bingo giggled.

Next day, Bingo went back to the cave. The burblies ate more of her food. She was amazed to see them climbing up the slippery walls using the pads on their fingers and toes.

Bingo didn't tell anyone about the strange new creatures, not even her grandfather.

Chapter 2

Every day after that, Bingo walked past the noisy diggers to the waterfall. The burblies soon rushed down to greet her when she arrived. They sat on her shoulders. The baby burblies fell asleep in her arms. The mummy

and daddy burbly showed her how they drank from the waterfall using their long tongues.

On her way to see the burblies one morning, Bingo was pleased to find the diggers had gone. But the workers who drove the diggers had been busy. They had left behind a vast, silent wall. It towered above the trees and cut across the river. Bingo noticed that the river wasn't flowing so quickly any more.

That night, she told her grandfather about the wall. He said it was called a 'dam'. "It doesn't belong here," he said. "The people who built it want to block the river so they can use the water."

Over the next few days, the river got narrower and narrower. The waterfall got smaller and smaller until it was just a trickle. The burblies' cave started to dry out.

Without the waterfall to protect them, the burblies were afraid. One morning, Bingo found the daddy burbly sitting in a tree making a loud booming call through his nose. It echoed across the forest.

The mummy and two baby burblies were huddling on the floor at the back of the cave. Their fur and skin had dried out. The cave walls were too dry for them to climb.

“You’re not safe here any more,” said Bingo. “I’ll take you home with me.”

Chapter 3

All the villagers crowded round to see the strange new creatures. Bingo built them a shelter down by the stream where it was cool and damp.

Bingo's friend Mingu made a cage. She wanted to keep a burbly as a pet in her house. But Bingo said: "No, they need to be wet."

The headman wanted to eat one for dinner. But Bingo said: “No, they are not for eating.”

Soon, news of the creatures spread through the jungle.

People from nearby villages came to see them. A man with a camera came. He took photos to put in the newspaper.

After that, a group of people with pale skin and bright-coloured clothes came to take more photos. Grandfather frowned at them from the doorway of his hut.

A big round man offered lots of money for the burblies. He wanted to put them in a zoo. But Bingo said: "No, they belong in the jungle."

A kind man in a blue shirt came to see them. His friend filmed him on a big camera while he crouched next to the burblies and whispered. The kind man patted Bingo on the head and said: "Take good care of them."

A scientist came next. She asked Bingo lots of questions about the burblies. Grandfather stood nearby and listened. The scientist prodded the burblies and took clippings of their fur.

"They don't like that," said Bingo.

"They are very special creatures," said the scientist. "I need to do some tests. Tomorrow I'll come back to take them away. Then you can help me find some more."

"There aren't any more," said Bingo.

Chapter 4

That night, Bingo couldn't sleep. She was worried about what would happen to the burblies.

As she tossed and turned on her sleeping mat, she heard a tap-tap-tap outside. It was her grandfather.

"Bring the burblies and follow me," he said.

Bingo followed her grandfather out of the village and into the dark forest. The burblies clung tightly around her neck.

It was pitch black among the trees, but Grandfather knew the way. The forest was full of strange sounds. All around them, frogs, bats, birds and insects were calling to each other.

Bingo and her grandfather climbed steadily up the mountain behind their village.

When the sun came up, they were high above the clouds. They stopped to eat some berries and fruit for breakfast. Grandfather watched as Bingo fed the burblies.

Then they walked all day. They walked down into the next valley and up the mountain on the other side, then down and up again.

All day, Grandfather told Bingo about the secrets of the forest. He showed her plants that could cure sickness. He showed her a bird that looked like a branch. He showed her frogs that had see-through skin.

They spent another night sleeping in the forest. The next day they walked again.

Chapter 5

On the third morning, Bingo and her grandfather scrambled down a steep rocky slope into yet another valley. The trees in this valley were taller and greener than any they'd seen before. Rivers raced down the mountains on all sides.

Just then, Bingo heard a distant booming noise. The daddy burbly, who was dozing on her shoulder, sat up.

The booming sound came again. The daddy burbly gave this own loud booming call. A boom came back in reply.

Bingo looked at her grandfather open-mouthed. He smiled back at her.

They walked down into the lush trees. A curtain of creepers blocked their way. Grandfather pushed the creepers aside and led Bingo into the most beautiful valley she had ever seen.

Waterfalls tumbled on all sides into a deep lake. There was a cool mist in the air, and rainbows filled the sky. The trees were bursting with flowers and fruits and berries. But some of the fruits were moving. Bingo looked closely and realised that they weren't fruits at all – they were burblies!

"Welcome to the Valley of a Thousand Rivers," said Grandfather. "My own grandfather brought me here a long time ago, when I was about your age."

He lifted his hands to his lips and gave a booming burbly call. Hundreds of burblies boomed back in reply. The four burblies on Bingo's shoulders joined in too. More burblies appeared from behind the waterfalls.

Bingo felt happy, but sad at the same time. She grinned at her furry friends.

"You're home now," she said. "I think you'll be safe here."

The burbly family gave her a big sticky hug. Then she held up her hands and let them climb into the nearest tree.

Grandfather put his arm around Bingo's shoulder. "Let's keep this place our little secret, shall we?" he said.

In the valley all around them, burblies burbled happily, just as they had done for hundreds of years.

The End

Book Bands for Guided Reading

Pink
Red
Yellow
Blue
Green
Orange
Turquoise
Purple
Gold
White

The Institute of Education book banding system is a scale of colours that reflects the various levels of reading difficulty. The bands are assigned by taking into account the content, the language style, the layout and phonics. Word, phrase and sentence level work is also taken into consideration.

Maverick Early Readers are a bright, attractive range of books covering the pink to white bands. All of these books have been book banded for guided reading to the industry standard and edited by a leading educational consultant.

To view the whole Maverick Readers scheme, visit our website at
www.maverickearlyreaders.com

Or scan the QR code above to view our scheme instantly!